THE LEGEND OF THE WHALE

THE LEGEND OF

THE WHALE

Ian Stansfield

Published by

David Bateman Ltd

This book is dedicated to the memory of Rudy Komon of the Rudy Komon Gallery, Sydney, and E. B. (Barney) Joyce, O.B.E.
My thanks to Lee-Anne Sinton for all her support.

©Ian Stansfield

First Published in 1985 by David Bateman Ltd
58 Townsend Court, Buderim 4556,
Queensland, Australia
In association with David Bateman Ltd
New Zealand

National Library of Australia
Cataloguing-in-Publication data

Stansfield, Ian
LEGEND OF THE WHALE

ISBN 0 908610 54 8

I. Title

A823'.3

Typeset in 14pt Garamond Light by Rennies Illustrations Ltd, Auckland and printed in Hong Kong by Everbest Printing Co. Ltd

Design and Production by David Bateman Ltd

Foreword

I only ever saw the Land of the Three Moons once and I know that I'll never see it again. It was then I learnt of the Legend of the Whale which I should like to share with you.

The Land of the Three Moons lies between the Minal and Three Moon Creeks in a valley which no man will see again. The moons never leave the sky, but change colour throughout the course of the day. As the colours of the moons change, so the trees, hills, and life itself merge in one continuous parade.

One night as the animals played and laughed together by the river, they were startled by the sight of Mungungo, Messenger of the Great Wockatoo, Lord of the Universe. Three tiny whales swam from the shimmering reflections of the moons. The animals stared in amazement as the voice of Mungungo echoed through the land.

'Animals of the Land of the Three Moons, it is the wish of the Great Wockatoo that you care for these whales and help them on their journey.'

Elephants trumpeted and birds sang farewell as the Messenger flew beyond the moons. Word of the miracle was sent to the Timeless Lizard without delay.

The Timeless Lizard was deep in meditation between the Red Rocks. It was said that the rocks had been brought from the Land of the Sun by the Great Wockatoo himself when he created the Land of the Three Moons. They had given the Lizard much wisdom, a true understanding of the Universe, and the ability to live forever. He stored all of this knowledge beneath his scales.

The animals all gathered round in silence as the Lizard began to speak about the birth of the whales.

He told how the Great Wockatoo would one day send the whales out into the world as a test to see if its inhabitants were ready for lasting peace. If all the whales were killed and their spirits returned to him, the Great Wockatoo would destroy the world for the benefit of other life in the Universe.

Having spoken, the Lizard sank back beneath the Red Rocks and the animals wandered back into the forest lost in thought.

The animals became great friends with the whales, and each evening would gather by the river to watch them as they basked and played in the moonlight. Hardly a conversation passed without someone remarking how big the whales were becoming. No one seemed to know how they could grow so fast, as they did not appear to feed on anything. A troop of mischievous monkeys spread a rumour that they were feeding on the moonlight. This satisfied everyone, apart from the Timeless Lizard, who thought it was a great joke.

By the end of the first year the whales had become so huge that they began to run aground every now and then in the shallows. It was clear to the whales that the Land of the Three Moons was not to be their home. So the whales and the animals held a council and hatched an ingenious plan.

The blue-spotted tapir hastily scurried off into the forest in search of the animals needed to carry out the plan. He returned with four strong elephants and three of the cleverest monkeys laden with jungle vines. Using all their skill, the monkeys soon made a harness from the vines.

The whales struggled and thrashed about until the harness held them securely. Two elephants were sent to each side of the river. The monkeys scrambled up their tails and tied the vines round their thick necks. Finally all was ready, and on a command from the blue-spotted tapir the elephants pulled with all their might, until the whales began to move.

A bird flew from the river bank and stood on the first whale's head to watch for submerged logs and rocks. The elephants had to summon all their strength to haul the whales through the shallow waters, and were exhausted by the time they arrived at a deep pool. When the whales were released from their harness they thanked the elephants by flicking water on them with their giant tails.

The whales swam freely without fear of being stranded in shallow waters, but they longed to dive deep into the seas and swim the great oceans. To their dismay, the way into the Great River was blocked by waterfalls which towered high above them. They swam round at the foot of the falls in despair. Their natural instinct to find their real home was clear to all the animals but they could do nothing to help them.

'We can't assist you,' shouted the blue-spotted tapir. 'Our only hope is that the Timeless Lizard can!'

The Lizard was tired, having recently returned from a long journey in search of knowledge. Just as he was dozing off between the Red Rocks, word of the whales' plight reached him.

'Hmmm,' said the Lizard at first, and then, 'every problem has its solution.' Nothing seemed to trouble the Lizard very much.

He set off slowly for the falls, taking long rests while he searched his scales for an answer. They told him that only a little water from the great river went over these falls — the rest flowed in a different direction to the Great Sea. If he could raise the water below the falls then it would reverse the flow and join the main river. Then the whales would be able to swim to the sea. So by the time he arrived he knew what had to be done. When the animals had calmed down, he walked to the water's edge and told them about the Rainbirds.

Even the waterfalls fell silent to listen to the Timeless Lizard. He told them of a place far away over the mountains that surrounded the Land of the Three Moons, a place called the Kingdom of the Sun. It was a vast, dry land, with neither rivers nor lakes, a land which would have died long ago, had it not been for the Rainbirds.

The Great Wockatoo had given them the power to make rain by performing a magic dance in the skies. The Temple of the Rainbirds lay in the centre of a hot, dry plain, on a great red mountain marked with a gigantic symbol of a lizard on its eastern side. It could be seen from a vast distance because of the fluffy white clouds which always hovered above it.

The Timeless Lizard asked for the swiftest bird in the land to take a message from him to the Rainbirds.

It was an unlikely-looking bird who came forward.

'My name is Cania. I will go,' she said without fear.

Everyone was surprised to see such a thin, ungainly creature volunteer for the difficult task which lay ahead. The Timeless Lizard raised his eyebrows, realising that Cania would not be strong enough to fly over the mountains and across the vast dry land. But he blessed her for her courage, conferring upon her an eagle's strength and the speed of the wind.

Soon Cania was soaring high above the valley and over the tops of the mountain ranges. Before her lay a sea of rolling red hills. Far in the distance she saw the clouds atop the mountain, about which the Timeless Lizard had spoken.

The Kingdom of the Sun was far different from anything Cania had seen before and she wondered how the animals could survive at all in the red land. She was close to exhaustion as she came over the last rise. The sun was just setting on the mountain and the clouds were high above. With a final burst of energy she soared high into the sky far above the mountain and then glided gracefully into the Temple of the Rainbirds.

She came to rest next to a spring and found herself surrounded by beautiful Rainbirds. The pool was clear as crystal and reflected the sky like a mirror. The Rainbirds welcomed her to their temple and invited her to drink the water which made her feel as though she had not flown at all.

She told the Rainbirds the story of the whales, and how she had been sent to ask their help by the Timeless Lizard. The Rainbirds were only too pleased to offer their assistance. While they made ready to fly to the Land of the Three Moons, one of them answered Cania's questions about the Kingdom of the Sun.

'A long time ago,' said the Rainbird, 'the Great Wockatoo made the Kingdom of the Sun. He was so tired at having made all the other lands of the world first, that as he flew across the sky with the sun held between his feet, it slipped. And so it was that the sun came much closer than had been intended, scorching and burning the Earth. Seeing the land so parched, he created us before all other living things, and showed us the magic of the Rain Dance. With the power to make rain, we must fly over all our land and dance in the sky to bring water to the animals and trees.'

'It must be a very tiring task indeed,' said Cania as she went to cool herself off in the pool.

'Indeed it is, for the land is so vast, we make just enough water to keep everything alive,' replied the Rainbird. 'The others are in readiness to return with you now. May the Great Wockatoo speed you home.'

They flew out from the mountain in a splendid colourful procession.

As the Rainbirds sped swiftly through the sky, listening to Cania's tales of the Land of the Three Moons, they were filled with excitement about what they might see. The long journey across the rolling plains passed quickly. Crossing over the high mountain range, they swooped down into the valley of the Three Moon Creek and the Rainbirds were stunned by its beauty and the changing colours of the sky and land.

A welcoming party of animals and birds surrounded the Timeless Lizard and watched as the majestic formation of Rainbirds landed by the waterfalls.

The Lizard greeted them warmly and then said, 'Our friends the whales must get to the Great River which leads to the sea, but the falls block their way. Would you be kind enough to dance in the sky and make it rain, until the river rises and the whales can swim over the falls?'

'It will be an honour to dance in the sky of the Three Moons,' said the Rainbirds.

In an instant the birds were in the air dancing amongst the moons, and it was not long before the clouds began to form and the rain came down with a force that shook the ground. Then they farewelled the animals before journeying home with some speed to keep their own land alive.

For many days and nights it rained and slowly the river began to swell. The animals all retreated to the high ground and watched as the water level rose, covering the lower hills and trees.

The whales swam impatiently round the waterfalls, anxious to be on their way to the sea. They realised they would never return and sang with all the joy and sorrow in their hearts a song they still sing today. Mungungo, Messenger of the Great Wockatoo, flew across the sky, encircling the centre moon and surrounding it with a sign that the Great Wockatoo was pleased and it held the promise of protection and eternal peace for the Land of the Three Moons.

As the next day dawned the water rose above the falls and the whales swam out into a new land. They glanced back to make a final farewell to all those who had helped them, just in time to see the Three Moons vanish into thin mist.

The journey down the Great River was a fast one and they raced through the rushing, bubbling water on their way to the sea. They were happy to be free and laughed so hard they blew holes in their heads and water poured out of them.

Everything they looked at was in vivid colour, for they now possessed the special vision of all who have ever been to the Land of the Three Moons.

At the mouth of the Great River was a maze of small islands and it was through these that the whales swam. Birds came in droves to see them and marvel at their strange shape and size. As they neared the ocean, the taste of salt caused such a state of excitement that the water again poured out of their heads in a tremendous torrent. The curious birds thought the whales were sinking, until they saw them leaping from the water and heard their cries of joy.

Out in the open sea the whales found the horizon endless and for the first time in their lives felt small in the vastness of the ocean.

'Where should we go?' said one whale.

'What shall we do?' said another.

'Why are we here?' asked the third.

For many days they swam backwards and forwards chasing the sun until they realised they were getting nowhere. They felt lost and sad, but never gave up hope of discovering the reason for their being in the great sea.

One day Mungungo appeared, laughing, out of the blue sky, and shouted down to the, 'If you're feeling lost, you'd better come with me.'

The whales turned and followed Mungungo as he flew away from the sun.

They swam far out to sea until a speck in the distance turned out to be a tiny island. As they drew closer they saw before them the Great Wockatoo himself and they were filled with awe.

The Great Wockatoo smiled down at them and said, 'I am well pleased with you, my whales, for you have found your way to the sea.'

'Yes,' said one of the whales, 'but now we are here, what is our purpose?'

The Wockatoo replied, 'I have made you the strongest of all my creatures as a lesson that strength and gentleness can go hand in hand. Let us hope that others learn this lesson from you. Many of you will die for it, but I will make a home for your spirits in the seas around my island.'

The whales turned and swam towards the horizon, happy that they knew what to do.

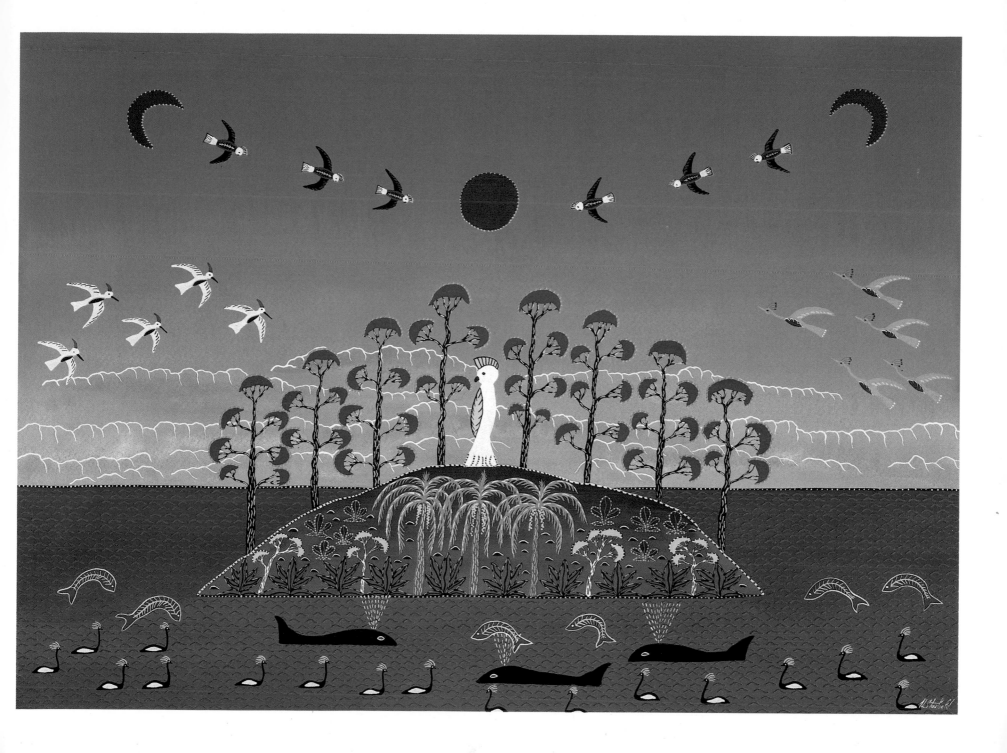

As time passed back in the Land of the Three Moons the animals wondered what had happened to the whales. One day they went to the Timeless Lizard and asked if he could tell them.

The Timeless Lizard saw the concern on their faces and said, 'I can only tell you what I know. It will take many hundreds of years for people to realise the lesson the whales were sent to teach. Whales will die, unable to protect themselves from the greed of others, but eventually the killing will stop.'

The animals smiled and nodded at each other, knowing that this meant the Earth would be saved from destruction. The Timeless Lizard scratched his scales and the watching animals imagined that he rippled like the ocean in the soft light of the moons.

THE END